SPOTTER'S GUIDE TO
THE NIGHT SKY

Nigel Henbest MSc FRAS
and Stuart Atkinson

Edited by Philippa Wingate
Designed by Nickey Butler
Series and cover designer: Laura Fearn

First published in 2000 by Usborne Publishing Ltd.,
Usborne House, 83-85 Saffron Hill, London, EC1N 8RT,
England. www.usborne.com

Printed in Spain

This picture shows the Moon reflected in the
waters of Lake Tanganyika, Africa, at sunrise.

CONTENTS

4 How to use this book
6 Out spotting
8 The Universe
10 Stars of the
   northern skies
12 Stars of the
   southern skies
14 Draco to Cancer
16 Cygnus to Serpens
18 Camelopardalis
   to Aquarius
20 Gemini to Lepus
22 Columba to
   Microscopium
24 Corvus to Dorado
26 Sagittarius to Crux
28 Birth of stars
30 Types of stars
32 Dying stars
34 Galaxies
36 Empire of the Sun

38 Mercury
39 Venus
40 Mars
41 Jupiter
42 Saturn
43 Uranus, Neptune,
   Pluto
44 Comets
45 Asteroids
46 The Moon
48 Phases of the Moon
49 Eclipses
50 Meteors
52 Other sky sights
53 Artificial satellites
54 Astronomy on-line
56 Taking photographs
57 Useful words
58 Scorecard
62 Index
64 Acknowledgements

HOW TO USE THIS BOOK

This book is an identification guide to the things you can see in the night sky. Take it with you when you go out spotting. Over a period of about a year, you should be able to see most of the things in this book that are visible from where you live.

WHAT TO LOOK FOR

You can find out which constellations will be visible using the sky map on page 10 (or page 12 if you live in the southern hemisphere). Look to see where the planets will be (pages 38-42), and find out about comets and asteroids (pages 44 and 45).

NEAR AND FAR

Some objects, like the stars, are very distant, while the planets, comets and the Moon are much closer. This book starts with the distant sky sights, then moves to ones closer to Earth, with descriptions to help you identify them.

MAKE YOUR MARK

Next to most of the things in the book is a circle. Whenever you spot an

object, make a mark in the circle. Some things, like the more distant planets, can only be seen using extremely powerful telescopes, so these don't have circles next to them.

There is a scorecard at the back of the book. Give yourself a score for each of the things you see.

	Score	Date spotted
Carina (**S**)	10	20/07/00
Cassiopeia (**N**)	5	
Centaurus (**S**)	5	26/06/00
Cepheus (**N**)	15	17/07/00
Cetus (**N**)	15	16/07/00
Chameleon (**S**)	20	20/07/00

The letter N or S next to an object indicates that it is visible only in the northern or southern hemisphere.

Planet Earth photographed from space

OUT SPOTTING

When you go out spotting, make sure you are well prepared. This section tells you what you'll need.

WHAT TO TAKE

- this book
- warm clothing, because you'll get cold when sitting still, even in summer
- a flashlight for looking at the star maps in this book
- binoculars or a telescope
- a notebook and pencil to record what you see
- a chair or mat to sit on, as standing up soon becomes uncomfortable.

IN THE DARK

Your eyes will take about 20 minutes to adapt to the darkness, so wait for a while before you try to spot the fainter stars. Use your flashlight to read the star maps in this book. The flashlight's glare can keep you from seeing well in the dark, so take care not to look directly at the light.

TAKE CARE

Don't go out in the dark alone. Go with a parent or guardian, or members of your astronomy club. (See page 55 for details of clubs and organizations to contact.)

Star maps help you to find your way around the night sky.

Eyepiece   Focusing
             control

Lightweight
binoculars are
easier to hold
still than big,
heavy ones.

BINOCULARS

You can see most of the
sights in this book with
your unaided eyes, but
you'll see much more
with a pair of binoculars.

Visit a good shop and
try out several pairs. A
pair of 7x50 binoculars
are ideal for looking at
the stars. Don't buy a
pair more than 10x50
or they will be too heavy.

TELESCOPES

Telescopes are more
powerful than binoculars,
but more expensive.
Many of the cheaper
ones are not very good.
For the cost of a cheap
telescope, it's better
to buy a good pair
of binoculars.

Eyepiece

Your telescope will need a
mount. Without one, you
will not be able to hold the
telescope still enough to
see anything.

THE UNIVERSE

The Universe is the name given to the collection of all things that exist in space. It's made up of millions of stars, planets, and vast clouds of gas.

LIGHT YEARS

Distances in space are huge, so astronomers measure them in "light years". One light year (LY) is the distance light travels in a year – 9.46 million million* km (5.88 million million* miles). Light travels at a speed of 300,000 km (186,000 miles) per second.

GALAXIES

Vast groups of stars are called galaxies. Earth is in the Milky Way galaxy. Astronomers think it contains about 100,000 million stars.

The Milky Way is a vast, spiral-shaped galaxy.

THE SUN

A star is a ball of hot gas which produces heat and light from a nuclear reaction within its core. The closest star to Earth is the Sun. After the Sun the nearest star is Proxima Centauri, 4.3 LY away.

THE EARTH

The Earth is one of nine planets which orbit (go around) the Sun. Together, the Sun and everything that orbits it are called the Solar System. The Earth takes one year to orbit the Sun. As it orbits, it spins, making a complete spin once a day.

* Trillion in the USA

SATELLITES

Any object in space that orbits around another is called a satellite. The Moon is a satellite that orbits the Earth once every 27.3 days. It is the Earth's only natural satellite. Most of the other planets have natural satellites.

THE BIG BANG

Many scientists think the Universe began about 15,000 million years ago in an enormous explosion, known as the Big Bang. Gas clouds thrown out by the explosion turned into galaxies. Even today, the galaxies are racing apart from each other as a result of the explosion.

THE BIG BANG THEORY

The Big Bang created a huge fireball. As this cooled, it began to spread out.

Thick clouds of gases began to form into vast, dense clumps of matter.

Stars and galaxies were gradually formed from this matter.

9

STARS OF THE NORTHERN SKIES

On a clear night you can see about 3,000 stars in the sky. Astronomers find their way around by grouping the stars into patterns, called constellations.

The best time to use the star map is around 11:00pm. Spotting some of the constellations can be tricky. It is best to choose a dark place on a dark, clear night.

USING THE STAR MAP
Turn the book around until the current month is nearest to you. Face south and look for the stars as they appear on the map. You should be able to see most of the stars in the middle and lower part of the map.

When you have found the constellations shown here, turn to the larger-scale maps on the following pages. The black lines on this map show the areas covered by each double-page. The page numbers to look up are marked in each section.

SEPTEMBER

AUGUST

JULY

JUNE

MAY

Aquarius

Equuleus

Pegasus

Delphinus

page 16-17

Vulpecula

Cygnus

Aquila

Lyra

Scutum

Serpens
Cauda

Hercules

Ophiuchus

Corona
Borealis

Serpens
Caput

Boötes

page 14-15

10

NOVEMBER

DECEMBER

JANUARY

FEBRUARY

MARCH

APRIL

Cetus

page 18-19

Pisces

Andromeda

Aries

Eridanus

page 22-23

Triangulum

Persus

Taurus

Lacerta

Cepheus

Cassiopeia

Camelopardalis

Orion

Ursa Minor

Lynx

Auriga

Gemini

Ursa Major

Draco

Canis Minor

page 20-21

Canes Venatici

Cancer

Monoceros

Leo Minor

Hydra

Coma Berenices

Leo

Virgo

Sextans

page 24-25

Use this map if you are star spotting in the northern hemisphere.

On this map, stars that are easy to see are shown larger than the less obvious ones. The white band on the map is the Milky Way.

11

STARS OF THE SOUTHERN SKIES

If you live in the southern hemisphere, use this map to find your way around the skies.

Turn the map until the current month is nearest you. Face north, and you should be able to see most of the stars shown in the middle and lower part of the map.

When you look at Sagittarius, you are also looking toward the middle of the Milky Way galaxy, so you will see lots of stars in that area of the sky. To the south you can see the Southern Cross, Crux.

When you have found the constellations shown here, turn to the larger-scale maps on the following pages. The black lines on this map show the areas covered by each double-page. The page numbers to look up are marked in each section.

The maps on the following pages only show the approximate positions of stars and galaxies.

JULY

AUGUST

SEPTEMBER

OCTOBER

NOVEMBER

Aquila

Equuleus

Capricornus

Pegasus

Microscopi

Aquarius

Piscis

Australis

page 18-19

Sculptor

Pisces

Cetus

JUNE

MAY

Use this map if you are star spotting in the southern hemisphere.

Ophiuchus

page 16-17

Serpens Caput

Scutum

APRIL

page 14-15

agittarius

Scorpius

Libra

Virgo

Telescopium

page 26-27

Ara

Norma

Lupus

Centaurus

orona

Triangulum

Cirinus

Corvus

MARCH

ustralis

Austale

Crater

ndus

Musca

Crux

Apus

Pavo

Octans

Chameleon

Soxtans

Tucana

Hydrus

Antila

Mensa

Volanis

Vela

Horologium

Carina

Pyxis

Hydra

ix

Reticulum

Pictor

page 24-25

Dorado

Puppis

FEBRUARY

Columba

Canis Major

Caelum

Fornax

Lepus

Monoceros

Eridanus

page 20-21

page 22-23

JANUARY

Orion

The size of each star symbol shows how bright the star is, not its actual size.

DECEMBER

13

DRACO TO CANCER

○ **1 DRACO (DRAGON)**
A long, straggling line of faint stars. Its "head" is a group of four stars near Vega; the "tail" loops around Ursa Minor (see no. 6 below).

○ **2 CANES VENATICI (HUNTING DOGS)**
This constellation was named in 1650. The "dogs" hunt the "bears", following them across the sky.

○ **3 BOÖTES (HERDSMAN)**
A kite shape. Arcturus is the fourth brightest star in the sky. Find it using the curved handle of the Plough (see no.8 below) as a pointer.

○ **4 COMA BERENICES (BERENICE'S HAIR)**
A cloud of faint stars. Binoculars will show about 30 of them.

○ **5 VIRGO (VIRGIN)**
A constellation representing the goddess of justice. Spica is a hot, bright white star.

○ **6 URSA MINOR (LITTLE BEAR)**
Polaris, the pole star, is important to navigators because it is always due north.

○ **7 LYNX**
A line of faint stars. Very hard to see.

Vega links to the map on page 17.

Nu Draconis

1

6

Kocab

Thuban

The Plough

Alcor and Mizar

3

To Arcturus

2

M3

Arcturus

4

To Spica

To Spica

5

Porrima

Spica

14

Polaris, the pole star
North celestial pole

To Polaris

M82
M81

Dubhe
Two end stars
point to Polaris
Merak

8

9

11
The Sickle

Praesepe

10

Regulus

Denebola

8 URSA MAJOR (GREAT BEAR)
A large constellation whose brightest stars make the "Plough". The two right-hand Plough stars, Dubhe and Merak, point to the pole star.

9 LEO MINOR (SMALL LION)
A faint constellation, named in 1690 by German astronomer Johann Hevelius.

10 CANCER (CRAB)
Faint stars between Leo and Gemini (page 20). The distant star cluster Praesepe (beehive) is a dim blur to the eye, but is spectacular through binoculars.

11 LEO (LION)
Looks vaguely like a crouching lion.

Key:
- Galaxy
- Double star
- Open cluster
- Globular cluster

CYGNUS TO SERPENS

12 CYGNUS (SWAN)
The bright star Deneb forms one corner of the Summer Triangle, together with Vega and Altair. Binoculars show many faint stars in Cygnus.

13 DELPHINUS (DOLPHIN)
A compact constellation with a very distinctive shape. Delphinus' "tail" star is 950 LY away.

14 SAGITTA (ARROW)
Four stars make an arrow shape, between Cygnus and Aquila. This constellation is very faint, and isn't shown on the map.

15 CAPRICORNUS (GOAT)
A distorted triangle of faint stars. Giedi is a double star. The planet Neptune was in Capricornus when first discovered.

16 AQUILA (EAGLE)
The bright star Altair is easily recognized because of its two fainter flanking stars.

17 SCUTUM (SHIELD)
Faint constellation, visible against the Milky Way.

18 VULPECULA (FOX)
A very inconspicuous star group. Originally called the fox and goose.

Key:
○ Nebula
✷ Open cluster
◎ Galaxy
✶ Double star
⊙ Globular cluster
◉ Planetary nebula

Giedi

M30

15

19 LYRA (LYRE)
A small but easily spotted group. Vega is the fifth brightest star in the sky, 26 LY away.

20 OPHIUCHUS (SERPENT BEARER)
A very large group of stars forming a distorted circle.

21 HERCULES
A large constellation, but rather shapeless and difficult to recognize.

The "Summer Triangle" is visible in the northern hemisphere in summer, and the southern hemisphere in winter.

Deneb

12

M29

13

M27

14

Albireo

Col399

18

Altair

16

17

23

Vega

19

M92

M13

21

Arcturus links to the map on page 14.

22

Rasalhague

Rasalgethi

Serpens Cauda

Serpens Caput

20

M10

M12

23

M5

23

M62

Antares links to the map on page 27. This star appears in Scorpius.

22 CORONA BOREALIS (NORTHERN CROWN)
A semicircle of faint stars between Vega and Arcturus.

23 SERPENS (SERPENT)
Consists of two separate parts: Caput (head) and Cauda (tail) lying either side of Ophiuchus.

CAMELOPARDALIS TO AQUARIUS

○ **24 CAMELOPARDALIS (GIRAFFE)**
Hard to see these stars with the naked eye.

○ **25 PERSEUS**
Named after a Greek hero. Algol is two stars close together.

○ **26 ANDROMEDA**
Named after a mythical princess. This galaxy can be seen with the naked eye even though it Is over 2 million LY away.

○ **27 TRIANGULUM (TRIANGLE)**
A compact pattern of three faint stars.

○ **28 ARIES (RAM)**
Three main stars. Gamma Arietis is a double star.

○ **29 PISCES (FISHES)**
In myth, two fish tied together by a long ribbon.

○ **30 CETUS (WHALE)**
Mira is a red star in Cetus. It remains visible to the naked eye for six months of the year, then fades to invisibility.

○ **31 CEPHEUS**
In myth, Andromeda's father. Its brightest star is Alderamin.

○ **32 LACERTA (LIZARD)**
A zig-zag of very faint stars. It is hard to find.

Capella links to the map on page 21.

NCGC869 and NGC884

Algol

Pleiades

M33

Gamma Arieris

Mira

Diphda

Polaris links to the map on page 15.

31

Alderamin

33

Delta Cephei

Mu Cephei

M39

32

To Pegasus

26

Andromeda Galaxy

Square of Pegasus

34

M15

Enif

35

Western Fish (or Circlet)

36

Water Jug

Delta Equuleus

Helix

33 CASSIOPEIA
In myth, wife of Cepheus. W-shape is easy to spot. The two end stars can be used as pointers to Pegasus.

34 PEGASUS
Three stars and the end star of Andromeda make up the square of Pegasus.

35 EQUULEUS (FOAL)
Hard to spot, even on a clear night.

36 AQUARIUS (WATER CARRIER)
Represents a man pouring water. The most obvious stars are the central four making the "Water Jug".

Key:

⭕ Nebula

🌀 Galaxy

Open cluster

★ Double star

Planetary nebula

Globular cluster

19

GEMINI TO LEPUS

37 GEMINI (TWINS)
Castor is actually six stars very close together, but binoculars cannot separate them. The faint planets Uranus and Pluto were in Gemini when discovered.

38 CANIS MINOR (SMALL DOG)
In myth, the smaller of the two dogs of Orion the hunter. Procyon is the eighth brightest star in the sky, and at 11 LY, one of the closest to Earth.

39 MONOCEROS (UNICORN)
Inconspicuous and given its name in the 17th century, but worth "sweeping" with your binoculars for star clusters and nebulae.

40 CANIS MAJOR (LARGE DOG)
A compact group of bright stars. Sirius (the Dog Star) is the brightest star in the sky. Read more about it on page 31.

41 AURIGA (CHARIOTEER)
A curving line of stars ending in a distinct but faint triangle known as the Kids. Capella is the sixth brightest star in the sky and 42 LY from Earth.

Castor
The Twins
Pollux
37
Delta Gemini

Rosette Nebula
38
Procyon
NGC2244

The Winter Triangle

39
Lots of star clusters in this area

Sirius
40
M‹

Adara

Capella

The Kids

41

M38

M36

M37

Pleiades, or
the Seven
Sisters

Key:
Nebula
Open cluster
Double star

Alnath

M35

Hyades

Aldebaran

42

Betelgeuse

43

Orion's
Belt

Orion
Nebula

Rigel

44

42 TAURUS (BULL)
The star Aldebaran is the
bull's eye, and its head is
the Hyades star cluster.
The Pleiades star cluster is
in Taurus. It is also known
as the "Seven Sisters",
though most people can
only see six stars in the
cluster.

43 ORION
In myth, Orion was a
great hunter. Contains
more bright stars than
any other constellation,
including red Betelgeuse
and Rigel. Spot the Orion
Nebula just below the
three stars of the belt.

44 LEPUS (HARE)
In myth, Orion liked
to hunt hares.

COLUMBA TO MICROSCOPIUM

45 COLUMBA (DOVE)
A distinct group of stars lying near Canopus, named in 1679.

This is the lower part of Orion, and links to the map on page 21.

Rigel

46 HOROLOGIUM (PENDULUM CLOCK)
Only one star is easily visible in this constellation.

53 INDUS (INDIAN)
Lies between Pavo and Grus.

47 CAELUM (CHISEL)
Consists of a few very faint stars.

54 FORNAX (FURNACE)
Lies in a curve of Eridanus.

48 RETICULUM (NET)
A distinct little group of faint stars between Canopus and Achernar.

55 TUCANA (TOUCAN)
A group of faint stars, named in 1603 by Johann Bayer.

45

49 MENSA (TABLE MOUNTAIN)
The faintest constellation in the sky. Look for it on a very clear night.

56 ERIDANUS (RIVER ERIDANUS)
A winding line of stars, named after a mythological river. It ends at Achernar, the ninth brightest star in the sky.

50 HYDRUS (SMALL WATER SNAKE)
A large triangle lying between the misty patches of the Magellanic Clouds.

57 PHOENIX
Named in 1603 after the mythological bird which rises from its own ashes.

51 OCTANS (OCTANT)
Always due south, but has no bright star to match Polaris in the northern hemisphere.

58 SCULPTOR
Consists of very faint stars. It was first called the sculptor's workshop.

52 PAVO (PEACOCK)
Conspicuous group of faint stars. Kappa Pavonis is a variable star, changing from dim to bright and back again every 19 days.

59 PISCIS AUSTRINUS (SOUTHERN FISH)
Includes the star Fomalhaut, which is 24 LY from Earth.

60 GRUS (CRANE)
A conspicuous group, its brightest star is called Alnair.

61 MICROSCOPIUM (MICROSCOPE)
All the stars are extremely faint, with just one easily made out.

Key:

⭕ Nebula   ✴ Double star

🌀 Galaxy   ⚬ Globular cluster

56

56

Canopus
(links to map,
page 25)

47

54

46

56

58

Large
Magellanic
Cloud

48

Achernar

57

Fomalhaut

59

50

55

60

49

Small
Magellanic
Cloud

Alnair

51   Apus

+
South
celestial
pole

53

61

52

Kappa Pavonis

23

CORVUS TO DORADO

Spica links to the map on page 14.

○ **62 CORVUS (CROW)**
A distinct foursome of stars in a rather barren area of the sky.

○ **63 CRATER (CUP)**
Another group of four stars, like a fainter Corvus.

M83: Galaxy in Hydra

○ **64 ANTLIA (AIR PUMP)**
A triangle of faint stars, named in 1763.

This area is full of clusters and nebulae

○ **65 VELA (SAIL)**
Part of the ancient constellation of the ship of Argo. Carina and Puppis form the rest. Its outline is marked by bright stars; binoculars show fainter ones.

The constellation Crux, often called the Southern Cross, links to the map on page 27.

○ **66 CHAMELEON**
Four faint stars.

○ **67 VOLANS (FLYING FISH)**
A distinct group of faint stars, partly enclosed by Carina.

○ **70 PYXIS (COMPASS)**
A few faint stars between Vela and Puppis.

○ **68 SEXTANS (SEXTANT)**
A small group of faint stars between Leo and Hydra.

○ **71 PUPPIS (STERN)**
Another part of Argo, the ship in Jason's quest for the Golden Fleece. Many stars and nebulae are visible through binoculars.

○ **69 HYDRA (WATER SNAKE)**
The longest constellation in the sky. The "head" is a conspicuous small group of six stars. The constellation only contains one bright star, Alphard.

○ **72 CARINA (KEEL)**
A line of stars forming the bottom of the ship Argo. At one end is Canopus, 120 LY distant and the second brightest star in the sky

Regulus links to the map on page 15.

68

63

62

69

M68: Globular cluster in Corvus

Alphard

69

64

Pyxis

70

65

Sirius links to the map on page 20.

71

72

66

67

73

74

Canopus

Beta Pictoris

Tarantula Nebula

Large Magellanic Cloud

Key:
- Nebula
- Open cluster
- Galaxy
- Double star
- Globular cluster

73 PICTOR (EASEL)
The second brightest star, Beta Pictoris, may have planets of its own.

74 DORADO (SWORDFISH)
Includes the misty patch of the Large Magellanic Cloud.

SAGITTARIUS TO CRUX

○ *75* **SAGITTARIUS (ARCHER)**
A distinctive "teapot" shape of bright stars. The misty nebula M8 is a region where stars are forming.

○ *76* **CORONA AUSTRALIS (SOUTHERN CROWN)**
Faint stars in a curving group of stars.

○ *77* **TELESCOPIUM (TELESCOPE)**
A group of faint stars near the tail of Scorpius.

○ *78* **ARA (ALTAR)**
Lies between Alpha Centauri and the tail of Scorpius.

○ *79* **CIRCINUS (COMPASSES)**
Consists of three faint stars near Alpha Centauri. Named in the 18th century.

○ *80* **TRIANGULUM AUSTRALE (SOUTHERN TRIANGLE)**
An easily spotted triangle of bright stars, named in 1603. The brightest star is only 100 LY away.

○ *81* **APUS (BIRD OF PARADISE)**
An inconspicuous group of stars, named in 1603.

○ *82* **MUSCA (FLY)**
A group of faint stars next to the Southern Cross.

○ *83* **SCORPIUS (SCORPION)**
Bright stars outline a realistic scorpion shape. Antares is a very bright red star. Binoculars show many faint star clusters.

○ *84* **LIBRA (SCALES)**
Four faint stars form the main part of Libra.

○ *85* **LUPUS (WOLF)**
A distinctive pattern of bright stars, stretching from Alpha Centuri to Antares.

○ *86* **NORMA (LEVEL)**
A group of faint stars. The region is filled with star clusters, since part of Norma lies in the Milky Way.

○ *87* **CENTAURUS (CENTAUR)**
In myth, a centaur was a creature half-man, half-horse. Alpha Centauri is the third brightest star in the sky.

○ *88* **CRUX (SOUTHERN CROSS)**
Alpha and Gamma Crucis point to the south celestial pole (the point directly above the south pole on Earth).

M25

M20

Nunki

M21

M8 Lagoon
Nebula

75

Key:
◯ Nebula   ✦ Double star
✳ Open   Globular
   cluster   cluster

M6

76

Shaula

Antares

83

83

84

77

NGC6397

78

86

85

79

Alpha
Centauri

80

Omega Centauri
star cluster

81

87

Coalsack
Nebula

Gamma
Crucis

To south celestial pole

Alpha
Crucis

82

88

BIRTH OF STARS

New stars form inside huge clouds of swirling dust and gas called nebulae. Within them, nuclear reactions begin, and a new star is formed. At the core of a star like the Sun, the temperature is about 15 million °C (27 million °F).

These pages show some nebulae and star clusters. There are millions more, but the ones shown are visible as faint, fuzzy patches to the naked eye. Some star clusters stay together, many break up. The stars may end up single, like the Sun.

↑LAGOON NEBULA (page 27)
Large clouds made of hydrogen gas. The star which makes the gas glow is so deeply embedded in dust that it cannot be seen. This nebula is over 5,000 LY away.

↑PRAESEPE (page 15)
An easily spotted cluster, 40 LY across and about 525 LY from Earth. Most of the stars (about 200) are thought to be about 400 million years old. No glowing nebula of hydrogen gas is visible.

More often, the stars end up in a pair or a trio.

A number of new stars that are still close together is called an open cluster. Globular clusters look like a single faint star, but are made up of up to a million stars.

○ **LAGOON NEBULA**

○ **PRAESEPE**

○ **ORION NEBULA**

○ **PLEIADES**

↑ORION NEBULA (page 21)

This is a huge glowing cloud of gas. It can be seen clearly with the naked eye, from both the northern and southern hemisphere, in the middle of Orion. It is 5,700 LY from Earth.

↑PLEIADES (page 21)

This star cluster is made up of over 250 stars, and was formed about 60 million years ago. It is often called the Seven Sisters, though only six bright stars are visible to the naked eye.

TYPES OF STARS

Stars vary enormously in size, shade and temperature. New stars tend to burn bright and hot. They look blue or white. Older stars are cooler and shine less brightly, and can look orange or red.

At 5,000 million years old, our Sun is a "middle-aged" star. Stars the size of our Sun have a lifespan of about 10,000 years. Smaller stars, called dwarf stars, live longer.

Stars that are larger than our Sun are called giant stars. The biggest are called supergiant stars. They live for only a few million years.

This chart shows the shades and temperatures of some typical stars.

TEMPERATURE	EXAMPLES	SHADE
25,000°C 37,832°F	Spica	Blue-white
10,000°C 18,032°F	Sirius	White
6,000°C 10,832°F	Sun	Yellow
4,700°C 8,492°F	Pollux	Orange
3,300°C 5,972°F	Betelgeuse	Red

➡ ALGOL (page 18)

Algol is a variable star. Every three days, it dims for ten hours, but not because its light output changes. It is in fact a double star, and one of the pair periodically blocks off the light of the other, reducing the brightness. About half of all known stars occur in pairs like this.

⬅ SIRIUS (page 20)

Sirius, 8.6 LY from Earth, has a faint companion which is a white dwarf. You can't see the dwarf, but should have no problem finding Sirius. Sirius is known as the "Dog Star" as it is in Canis Major. It's the brightest star in the sky.

➡ MIZAR AND ALCOR (page 14)

Mizar, the second star in the "handle" of the Plough, has a companion star, Alcor, which can be spotted with the naked eye. Mizar itself is a double star, but the pair can only be seen with a telescope.

Alcor ➡ ⬅ Mizar

DYING STARS

Stars don't shine forever. Eventually their supply of gas runs out and they die. As they die, stars that are the size of our Sun (or smaller) swell up and turn red. They are then called red giants. Slowly they puff their outer layers of gas into space.

A small, almost dead star, called a white dwarf is left. It eventually cools and fades.

Stars that are bigger than our Sun have a spectacular death. They swell up into vast red stars known as red supergiants. Then they blow up with a huge explosion called a supernova.

Barnard's star is a dwarf star, cooler than our Sun.

The Sun is a yellow star.

This diagram compares the size of some bright stars, including our Sun.

Arcturus is in the constellation of Boötes (see page 14). It is a giant star.

Rigel, in the constellation of Orion (see page 21) is a supergiant star.

➡ BETELGEUSE (page 21)

A red giant, easily spotted at the "shoulder" of Orion. The star varies in brightness slowly. Its size varies with its brightness. At its maximum, it is nearly 700 million km (438 million miles) across, over 500 times as large as the Sun.

⬅ ANTARES (page 26)

Another old red giant, about 400 million km (250 million miles) in diameter. It has a small companion star which can only be seen with a telescope. The companion is greenish. Antares' surface temperature is only 3,300°C (5,972°F)

➡ MIRA (page 18)

The central star in the constellation of Cetus is a red giant whose brightness varies. Over months its brightness can increase about a thousand times.

33

GALAXIES

The stars you see in the sky are part of a spiral group of 100,000 million stars, called the Milky Way galaxy. You can only see a fraction of these stars.

Beyond the Milky Way are billions more galaxies. The light from the distant galaxies blends together to form a misty band stretching across the sky which passes through the constellations of Cygnus, Cassiopeia, Aquila, Vela, Sagittarius, Scorpius, Centaurus, Crux, Puppis, Monoceros and Perseus.

◀ MILKY WAY
This is a section of the Milky Way as seen through a telescope. Using binoculars, you may see faint nebulae and star clusters within it.

Dust particles in space absorb starlight, producing dark "holes" in the Milky Way. Look in the constellation of Orion for the Horse's Head Nebula shown here.

➡ ANDROMEDA GALAXY (page 19)

To the naked eye it looks like a faint blur. It is almost 2.2 million LY away and is the most distant object you can see without binoculars or a telescope. Its spiral shape is similar to that of the Milky Way. Galaxies group together in clusters. Andromeda is a member of the Local Group, along with the Milky Way, the Magellanic Clouds and about 25 other galaxies.

Large Magellanic Cloud

Small Magellanic Cloud

⬅ MAGELLANIC CLOUDS (pages 23, 25)

These bright misty patches, only visible from the southern hemisphere, were first spotted by the explorer Ferdinand Magellan in 1521. They are smaller than our galaxy. Neither of the clouds has a distinctive shape, which is unusual, because galxaies usually have a spiral or oval shape.

EMPIRE OF THE SUN

On a clear night you'll probably see one or more bright points of light that aren't marked on the star maps. These are planets.

All the planets revolve around the Sun in the same direction. They gradually change their positions against the background stars, so they can't be marked on the constellation maps. After each planet's description on the following pages, there is a table that tells you where and when to

The Solar System. The planets and the distances between them are not shown to scale.

Mercury

Earth

Venus

Mars

Sun

Jupiter

PLANETARY FACT-FINDER

PLANET	NUMBER OF MOONS	AVERAGE DISTANCE FROM THE SUN
Mercury	None	58 million km (36 million miles)
Venus	None	108 million km (68 million miles)
Earth	1	149 million km (93 million miles)
Mars	2	228 million km (143 million miles)
Jupiter	16	778 million km (486 million miles)
Saturn	18	1,429 million km (893 million miles)
Uranus	20	2,875 million km (1,797 million miles)
Neptune	8	4,500 million km (2,813 million miles)
Pluto	1	5,900 million km (3,688 million miles)

look for the planets during the next few years. The planets seem to move through the same groups of constellations, known as the zodiac. The zodiac consists of Pisces, Aries, Taurus, Gemini, Cancer, Leo, Virgo, Scorpius, Sagittarius, Capricornus, Libra and Aquarius.

Apart from Uranus, Neptune and Pluto, the planets appear very bright. Once you have located their constellations you can't miss them.

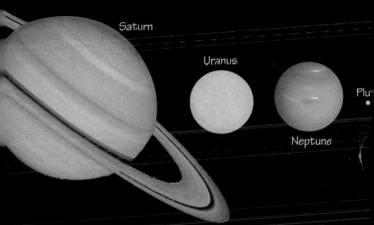

Saturn

Uranus

Pluto

Neptune

DIAMETER	TIME TO ORBIT SUN (A YEAR)	TIME TO SPIN ONCE (A DAY)
4,880km (3,050 miles)	88 days	59 days
12,104km (7,565 miles)	225 days	243 days
12,756km (7,972 miles)	365.3 days	23hrs 56 mins
6,794km (4,246 miles)	687 days	24hrs 37 mins
142,984km (89,365 miles)	11.9 years	9hrs 50 mins
120,536km (75,335 miles)	29.5 years	10hrs 14 mins
51,158km (31,974 miles)	84 years	17hrs 14 mins
49,532km (30,958 miles)	165 years	18 hrs
2,274km (1,421 miles)	248 years	6 days 10hrs

Mercury can only be seen low on the horizon in the twilight glow.

MERCURY

The diameter of Mercury, the closest planet to the Sun, is only 50% larger than that of the Moon. It has no atmosphere and during its day, the Sun bakes its surface up to 427°C (800°F). At night, its temperature can fall to −183°C (−300°F). Mercury is heavily cratered like the Moon, and has long ridges where it has shrunk slightly, like an old apple.

MERCURY – WHEN AND WHERE TO LOOK

YEAR	MORNING SKY	EVENING SKY
2000	August-November	February, June
2001	March, October	May, September
2002	March, July	May, August
2003	February, June	April, August, December
2004	January, September	March, July
2005	January, December	March, July

VENUS

Venus is a similar size to the Earth, but its atmosphere is a hundred times thicker and made of choking carbon dioxide. This thick blanket makes Venus' surface very hot – about 480°C (900°F). The planet is veiled by clouds made of sulphuric acid droplets. Space probes have shown that its surface has craters, mountains and valleys.

VENUS – WHEN AND WHERE TO LOOK

YEAR	MORNING SKY	EVENING SKY
2000	January-February	August-December
2001	April-November	January-March
2002	November-December	March-August
2003	January-March	November-December
2004	July-December	January-April
2005	January	June-December

Venus is the brightest object in the sky after the Sun and Moon. It appears as the "Evening Star" after sunset, or the "Morning Star" before sunrise.

Mars appears in the sky as a bright red "star".

MARS

Mars is a rocky planet, half the diameter of Earth. It has a thin atmosphere of unbreathable carbon dioxide, and has no liquid water on its surface. The entire surface, apart from icy polar caps, is a dry, red desert. Mars has canyons and volcanoes larger than any on Earth. One volcano, Olympus Mons, is 25km (16 miles) high and 500km (315 miles) across. Mars has two small moons, Phobos and Deimos.

MARS – WHEN AND WHERE TO LOOK

YEAR	MONTHS VISIBLE	CONSTELLATION	PAGE
2000	August	Cancer	15
	September-October	Leo	15
	November-December	Virgo	14
2001	January-February	Libra	27
	November-December	Capricorn	16
2002	April-May	Taurus	21
	October-December	Virgo	14
2003	January	Scorpius	26
	June-November	Aquarius	19
2004	January	Pisces	18
	February-April	Taurus	21
	December	Libra	27
2005	June-July	Pisces	18
	August-December	Aries	18

JUPITER

Jupiter is the largest planet in the Solar System. It spins faster than the Earth. On Jupiter, one day lasts less than 10 hours. The stripes visible through a telescope are cloud layers. Jupiter's most noticeable feature is the Great Red Spot. This is a huge storm that has been blowing for at least 300 years.

Jupiter appears as a bright yellowish-white point of light, brighter than any of the stars.

The Great Red Spot

JUPITER – WHEN AND WHERE TO LOOK

YEAR	MONTHS VISIBLE	CONSTELLATION	PAGE
2000	March-May	Aries	18
	October-December	Taurus	21
2001	January-April	Taurus	21
	October-December	Gemini	20
2002	January-May	Gemini	20
	August-November	Cancer	15
2003	January-May	Cancer	15
	October-December	Leo	15
2004	January-May	Leo	15
	November-December	Virgo	14
2005	January-May	Virgo	14

SATURN

The second largest planet in the Solar System is Saturn. It consists almost entirely of substances that are gases on Earth: ammonia, methane, hydrogen and helium. Inside Saturn, enormous gravity compresses these into liquids.

Saturn is famous for its rings. These consist of billions of ice particles which orbit Saturn like miniature moons. Saturn has 18 moons, the largest, Titan, has orange clouds.

Saturn appears to the naked eye as a bright yellow "star". Its rings are only visible through a telescope.

SATURN – WHEN AND WHERE TO LOOK

YEAR	MONTHS VISIBLE	CONSTELLATION	PAGE
2000	January-April	Aries	18
	October-December	Taurus	21
2001	January-April	Taurus	21
	August-December	Taurus	21
2002	January-April	Taurus	21
	August-December	Taurus	21
2003	January-April	Taurus	21
	Septermber-December	Gemini	20
2004	January-April	Gemini	20
	September-December	Gemini	20
2005	January-April	Gemini	20
	September-December	Cancer	15

URANUS, NEPTUNE, PLUTO

The three outer planets are not visible to the naked eye. Llittle was known about them until 1989, when the Voyager 2 spacecraft flew past Uranus and Neptune. It sent us detailed photographs of the planets and their rings and moons.

➡ URANUS
Discovered in 1781 by William Herschel. Uranus has 20 moons, more than any planet in the Solar System. Five small ones were discovered recently,

⬅ NEPTUNE
This planet is blue and similar to Uranus in size. It has two satellites, Nereid and Triton. Triton is one of the largest satellites in the Solar System at 2,720km (1,700 miles) In diameter.

➡ PLUTO
Only very powerful telescopes can show Pluto and Its large moon, Charon. Pluto's orbit passes inside that of Neptune, so that between 1979 and 1999, Neptune was the outermost planet.

COMETS

Comets are balls of ice, dust and rock. Some drift in huge orbits that extend far into space, even beyond the orbit of Pluto. As a comet nears the Sun, the heat turns the ice into a mini-atmosphere that streams out into a tail. One of the longest tails recorded was that of the Great Comet of 1843. It was about 330 million km (200 million miles) long. Sometimes a comet is large and bright enough to be seen without binoculars, but most are only visible through telescopes.

↑ HALLEY'S COMET
Of the comets that reappear regularly, the brightest is Halley's Comet, which reappears every 76 years. It will next appear sometime during 2061.

ASTEROIDS

Asteroids are large pieces of either rock, or rock and metal. Scientists believe they are bits and pieces that were left over when our Solar System formed. Many asteroids may measure over 100km (62 miles) across. However, only two (Vesta and Ceres) can be spotted with the naked eye.

Most asteroids orbit the Sun between Mars and Jupiter, in a region called the Asteroid Belt. Astronomers have recorded the orbits of about 4,000 asteroids, but they think there could be well over 10,000.

The distances between asteroids in the Asteroid Belt are huge. Spacecraft can pass through without hitting any of them.

DIAMETERS OF THE LARGEST ASTEROIDS

Ceres	932km (583 miles)
Vesta	538km (336 miles)
Pallas	522km (326 miles)
Hygeia	430km (269 miles)
Euphrosyne	370km (231 miles)

THE MOON

The Moon is Earth's only natural satellite. It is 3,476km (2,172 miles) in diameter, which is about a quarter the diameter of Earth. The Moon's surface is covered with craters, up to 250km (150 miles) across. The craters were blasted out by asteroids and meteorites millions of years ago. The Moon also has mountains, some almost 10km (6.5 miles) high.

The dark patches which spread over large areas of the Moon are plains of solidified lava. Early astronomers thought they were seas and oceans, and they still have the Latin names "mare" (sea) and "oceanus" (ocean).

The Moon always keeps the same side facing Earth. It turns around completely in 27.3 days, exactly the same time as it takes to orbit the Earth.

This picture of the Moon shows some of the main lunar features which are easy to spot with unaided eyes.

Mare Imbrium
Sea of Showers

Copernicus
A crater

Oceanus Procellarum
Ocean of Storms

Mare Nubium
Sea of Clouds

Mare Humorum
Sea of Humours

Tycho
A crater

MARE TRANQUILLITATIS
Sea of Tranquility

MARE SERENITATIS
Sea of Serenity

MARE FECUNDITATIS
Sea of Fertility

MARE VAPORUM
Sea of Vapours

MARE HUMORUM
Sea of Humours

MARE IMBRIUM
Sea of Showers

MARE NECTARIS
Sea of Nectar

MARE CRISIUM
Sea of Crises

MARE NUBIUM
Sea of Clouds

MARE FRIGORIS
Sea of Cold

COPERNICUS
A crater

TYCHO
A crater

OCEANUS PROCELLARUM
Ocean of Storms

Mare Frigoris
Sea of Cold

Mare Serenitatis
Sea of Serenity

Mare Crisium
Sea of Crises

Mare Vaporum
Sea of Vapours

Mare Tranquilitatis
Sea of Tranquility

Mare Fecunditatis
Sea of Fertility

Mare Nectaris
Sea of Nectar

PHASES OF THE MOON

The Moon emits no light of its own. Like the planets, it just reflects sunlight. As the Moon orbits the Earth, different amounts of the sunlit half are visible, so the lit shape (called the phase) changes. The phases repeat every 29½ days.

This diagram shows how the Moon's phases occur.

Direction of sunlight

The pictures below show what the Moon looks like from Earth when it is in each of the numbered positions above.

1 New moon   **2** Crescent   **3** Half Moon   **4** Waxing

5 Full Moon   **6** Waning   **7** Half Moon   **8** Crescent

THE MOON – FACTS AND FIGURES

Diameter	3,476km (2,172 miles)
Average distance from Earth	384,000km (240,250 miles)
Time taken to orbit Earth	27.3 days
Time to rotate once (lunar day)	27.3 days
Surface temperature by day	123°C (253°F)
Surface temperature by night	–123°C (–206°F)

ECLIPSES

← ECLIPSE OF THE SUN
This occurs when the New Moon passes in front of the Sun, cutting off its light. In a total eclipse the Sun's corona (outer atmosphere) can be seen.

This diagram shows the Moon sliding over the face of the Sun during a total eclipse of the Sun.

➡ ECLIPSE OF THE MOON
This occurs when the Full Moon passes into the shadow of the Earth. There is little light to reflect, so the Moon dims and looks coppery-brown.

This diagram shows the Moon in the Earth's shadow during an eclipse of the Moon.

NEVER LOOK AT THE SUN
Never look straight at a solar eclipse, or view it through smoked glass, or look at it through binoculars or a telescope. The rays from the Sun may blind you.

METEORS

Small pieces of debris floating around in the Solar System are called meteoroids. They range in size from enormous rocks to tiny grains of dust.

A photograph of a Perseid meteor shower (see the table on page 51)

METEORS

When meteoroids fall into the Earth's atmosphere, they burn up and make a bright streak across the sky. These are called meteors or shooting stars. On a clear night, you can see a few meteors every hour. A really bright meteor is called a fireball.

Fireball   Meteor

METEOR SHOWERS

Most small meteoroids are the remains of broken-up comets. When Earth passes through a stream of dust left by a comet, there are spectacular showers of meteors. You'll see dozens of meteors every hour. The table on the right gives information about when important meteor showers will occur.

METEORITES

Some meteors fall to the Earth as charred rocks. Once they hit the ground, these rocks are called meteorites. Look for them in museums.

↑ STONY METEORITE

There are two main types of meteorites, stony and iron. Stony ones are called aerolites. They are often covered with a smooth black crust.

← IRON METEORITE

Iron meteorites are also known as siderites. Examination under a microscope reveals a peculiar criss-cross pattern.

IMPORTANT METEOR SHOWERS

PEAK DATE	SHOWER NAME	FROM THE CONSTELLATION	NO. PER HOUR
Jan. 3/4*	Quadrantids	Left of Mizar/Alcor	up to 100
April 21	Lyrids	Lyra	up to 15
May 5	Eta Aquarids	Aquarius	up to 35
July 29	Delta Aquarids	Aquarius	up to 25
Aug. 12*	Perseids	Perseus	up to 80
Oct. 21	Orionids	Orion	up to 30
Nov. 17*	Leonids	Leo	variable
Dec. 13*	Geminids	Gemini	up to 100

Note: * indicates particularly good meteor showers.

OTHER SKY SIGHTS

In addition to planets and stars, there are other things to spot nearer the Earth.

⬇ AURORA BOREALIS/ AUSTRALIS

This shimmering curtain effect is caused by radiation from the Sun striking particles in Earth's upper atmosphere. Known as the Borealis in the northern hemisphere and Australis in the southern hemisphere. The aurorae can usually only be seen from areas in the far north and the far south of the Earth.

⬅ ZODIACAL LIGHT

A cone of light caused by sunlight reflecting off dust particles. The glow passes through the constellations of the zodiac. Best seen from tropics.

➡ HALO AROUND THE MOON

Caused by ice particles in the upper atmosphere. Usually only one silvery-white ring can be seen, but sometimes two.

ARTIFICIAL SATELLITES

Since the launch of Sputnik I in 1957, thousands of artificial satellites have been launched into orbit around the Earth. The largest ones can be seen with the naked eye. They look like slow, steadily moving points of silvery-white light. Beware of mistaking aircraft for satellites. Aircraft have red and blue identification lights on their wing-tips, and you can usually hear their engines on a quiet night.

TDRS Satellite

⬆ ARTIFICIAL SATELLITE

There are so many satellites that you will usually see one within an hour's spotting. As it passes into the Earth's shadow it will be eclipsed, fading out of sight. Some satellites flash because they are spinning in orbit. Sunlight reflects off different parts, causing a flashing effect.

Satellite

Flashing satellite

The Mir space station

⬅ SPACE STATIONS

Space stations orbit the Earth at a distance of about 400km (250 miles). They are laboratories where experiments can be done away from the effect of the Earth's gravity.

ASTRONOMY ONLINE

If you have a computer you can visit these Web sites to find out more about space. For links to the sites, go to the Usborne Quicklinks Web site at **www. usborne-quicklinks.com** and enter the keywords "spotters night sky".

WEB SITE 1 Visit the NASA multimedia gallery to see amazing space photographs, and video and audio clips sent back from space missions and telescopes.

WEB SITE 2 Visit the NASA Spaceflight Web site for masses of information about the Space Shuttles, Space Station and living in space.

WEB SITE 3 Send a question to an astronaut, or browse the archives of previously asked questions. The questions are answered by astronauts who have been on space missions, and you can find out what they eat, how they sleep when weightless, and see movies from the astronauts space missions.
To ask a question, fill in a form on the Web site, then visit the site in a few days' time to see if your question has been answered.

An astronaut makes a space walk.

(Above and right) Pictures of Mars that appeared on NASA's Web site in 1997.

Internet safety: When using the Internet, please follow the safety guidelines shown on the Usborne Quicklinks Web site.

WEB SITE 4 Go to the Kennedy Space Center for up-to-date news, Including a space shuttle launch countdown.

WEB SITE 5 Visit this Web site to find out how to observe the Space Shuttles or Space Station, or other events in space.

WEB SITE 6 Take a virtual, fly-by tour of the Sun with amazing close-up views of the planets.

WEB SITE 7 Take a multimedia tour of our solar system, and find out more about asteroids, meteors and spacecraft.

WEB SITE 8 View detailed star maps enriched with images from the Hubble Space Telescope.

ORGANIZATIONS TO JOIN
For links to the Web sites of these organizations, go to **www.usborne-quicklinks.com** and enter the keywords "spotters night sky".

The Royal Astronomical Society of Canada (RASC)
136 Dupont Street, Toronto, ON, M5R 1V2, Canada

British Astronomical Association (BAA)
Burlington House, Piccadilly, London, W1V 9AG, UK

Astronomical Society of the Pacific (ASP)
390 Ashton Avenue, San Francisco, California, 94112, USA

Royal Astronomical Society of New Zealand (RASNZ)
PO Box 3181, Wellington, New Zealand

The Astronomical Society of Australia (ASA)
Astronomy Department, School of Physics A28, University of Sydney, N.S.W., Australia 2006

TAKING PHOTOGRAPHS

You don't have to be an expert in photography to take some really good photos of the night sky.

SETTING UP YOUR CAMERA

You will need a single lens reflex (SLR) camera, which is a camera with a shutter that can be held open. Turn the focus ring until it is focused on infinity. Open the aperture to its widest setting – shown by the smallest "F" number.

To make sure the camera doesn't move when the picture is taken, place it on a wall or tripod. Ideally, you should use a shutter release cable to press the button.

Turn the focus ring until it is focused on infinity.

SLR camera

Open the aperture to its widest setting.

STAR TRAILS

Point your camera at any part of the sky. Keep the shutter open for at least ten minutes to get a result like the one shown here, as the stars rotate in the sky.

This picture shows star trails and an SLR camera, the best type of camera to take pictures of the night sky.

HANDY TIP

When you get your film processed, tell the assistant that the photos are of stars. Otherwise, it might be assumed that the results are mistakes and they may not be printed.

USEFUL WORDS

This glossary explains some of the terms used in this book. Words that appear in *italic* text are defined separately in the glossary.

asteroid – small rocky object orbiting the Sun. Thousands of them exist in the Asteroid Belt between Mars and Jupiter.

Big Bang – name given to the huge explosion which scientists think was the beginning of the Universe.

binary – two stars orbiting around each other.

eclipse – the total or partial blocking of one object in space by another. For example, in an eclipse of the Sun, the Sun is hidden by the Moon for a brief period.

galaxy – a giant group of stars. For example, the Milky Way galaxy contains about 100,000 stars.

hemisphere – half of a planet or moon. The top half is the northern hemisphere, the bottom half is the southern hemisphere.

Light Year – the distance light travels in a year. One light year (LY) is 9.46 million million* km (5.88 million million* miles).

meteor – a *meteoroid* that travels though Earth's atmosphere.

meteorite – a *meteoroid* that hits the Earth's suface.

meteoroid – a chunk of rock or dust flying in space.

nebula – cloud of dust and gas where new stars often form.

orbit – the path taken by one object as it revolves around another, for example, the planets orbit the Sun.

phases – different shapes that the moon and some planets seem to have as differing amounts of their sunlit sides are seen.

satellite – any object in space that orbits another object. Man-made satellites are launched into space to orbit the Earth.

star – a ball of constantly exploding gases, giving off light and heat.

sunspot – one of the dark patches that sometimes appear on the Sun.

white dwarf – tiny remains of a much larger star.

*Trillion in the USA

SCORECARD

After a night's spotting, write the date next to the objects you see in this scorecard. Keep a record of your nightly scores. The letter **N** or **S** next to an object indicates that it is visible only in the northern or southern hemisphere. Other objects, like meteorites, will usually be seen in museums, so score if you see them there.

	Score	Date spotted		Score	Date spotted
Aurora Australis (**S**)	35		Canes Venatici (**N**)	15	
Aurora Borealis (**N**)	35		Canis major	5	
Zodiacal light	40		Canis minor	10	
Artificial satellites Flashing satellite	15		Capricornus	15	
Satellite	5		Carina (**S**)	10	
Constellations Andromeda	5		Cassiopeia (**N**)	5	
Antlia (**S**)	15		Centaurus (**S**)	5	
Apus (**S**)	10		Cepheus (**N**)	10	
Aquarius	10		Cetus (**N**)	15	
Aquila	5		Chameleon (**S**)	20	
Ara (**S**)	15		Circinus (**S**)	20	
Aries	10		Columba (**S**)	15	
Auriga	5		Coma Berenices	15	
Boötes	5		Corona Australis (**S**)	10	
Caelum (**S**)	20		Corona Borealis	10	
Camelopardalis (**N**)	20		Corvus	10	
Cancer	10		Crater	15	

	Score	Date spotted		Score	Date spotted
Crux (**S**)	5		Monoceros	20	
Cygnus	5		Musca (**S**)	15	
Delphinus	10		Norma (**S**)	20	
Dorado (**S**)	15		Octans (**S**)	20	
Draco (**S**)	10		Ophiuchus	10	
Equuleus	20		Orion	5	
Eridanus	10		Pavo (**S**)	15	
Fornax (**S**)	20		Pegasus	5	
Gemini	5		Perseus (**N**)	10	
Grus (**S**)	15		Phoenix (**S**)	15	
Hercules	10		Pictor (**S**)	20	
Horologium (**S**)	15		Pisces	15	
Hydra (**S**)	15		Piscis Austrinus	15	
Hydrus (**S**)	15		Puppis	15	
Indus (**S**)	15		Pyxis (**S**)	20	
Lacerta (**N**)	15		Reticulum (**S**)	15	
Leo	5		Sagitta	15	
Leo minor (**N**)	15		Sagittarius	5	
Lepus	10		Scorpius	5	
Libra	15		Sculptor (**S**)	20	
Lupus (**S**)	15		Scutum	15	
Lynx (**N**)	15		Serpens	15	
Lyra	5		Sextans	20	
Mensa (**S**)	20		Taurus	5	
Microscopium (**S**)	20		Telescopium (**S**)	15	

	Score	Date spotted		Score	Date spotted
Triangulum	15		Mare Fecunditatis	15	
Triangulum Australe (S)	10		Mare Frigoris	15	
Tucana (S)	15		Mare Humorum	15	
Ursa major (N)	5		Mare Imbrium	10	
Ursa minor (N)	10		Mare Nectaris	15	
Vela	10		Mare Nubium	15	
Virgo	10		Mare Serenitatis	10	
Volans (S)	20		Mare Tranquillitatis	10	
Vulpecula	15		Mare Vaporum	15	
Eclipses: Lunar Partial	30		Oceanus Procellarum	5	
Total	40		Copernicus	10	
Eclipses: Solar Partial	50		Tycho	10	
Total	100		**Phases of the moon** New Moon	5	
Meteors Fireball	30		Crescent	5	
Meteor	20		Half Moon	5	
Iron meteorite	30		Waxing	5	
Stony meteorite	30		Full Moon	5	
Meteor showers Eta Aquarids	30		Waning	5	
Geminids	30		Halo around the Moon	15	
Lyrids	20		**Nebulae and star clusters**		
Orionids	25		Horse's Head Nebula	80	
Perseids	15		Lagoon Nebula	20	
Quadrantids	20		Orion Nebula	10	
Taurids	20		Pleiades (N)	10	
Moon Mare Crisium	10		Praesepe	15	

	Score	Date spotted		Score	Date spotted
Planets Jupiter	10		Andromeda Galaxy	15	
Mars	10		Antares	5	
Mercury	15		Betelgeuse	5	
Saturn	15		Magellanic Cloud (S)	10	
Uranus	20		Milky Way	5	
Venus	10		Mira	15	
Stars and galaxies Alcor (N)	10		Mizar (N)	5	
Algol (N)	20		Sirius	5	

NOTES

INDEX

Alcor, 31
Algol, 31
Andromeda, 18, 35
Antares, 33
Antlia, 24
Apus, 26
Aquarius, 19
Aquila, 16
Ara, 26
Arcturus, 32
Aries, 18
artificial satellites, 53
asteroids, 45
    Asteroid Belt, 45
Auriga, 20
Aurora Australis/Borealis, 52

Barnard's star, 32
Betelgeuse, 33
Big Bang, 9
Boötes, 14

Caelum, 22
Camelopardalis, 18
Cancer, 15
Canes Venatici, 14
Canis Major, 20
Canis Minor, 20
Capricornus, 16
Carina, 24
Cassiopeia, 19
Centaurus, 26
Cepheus, 18
Ceres, 45
Cetus, 18
Chameleon, 24
Charon, 43
Circinus, 26
Columba, 22
Coma Berenices, 14
comets, 44
Copernicus, 46
Corona Australis, 26
Corona Borealis, 17
Corvus, 24
Crater, 24
Crux, 12, 26

Cygnus, 16

Deimos, 40
Delphinus, 16
Delta Aquarids, 51
Dorado, 25
Draco, 14

Earth, 8, 36
Equuleus, 19
Eridanus, 22
Eta Aquarids, 51
Euphrosyne, 45

Fornax, 22

Galaxies, 8
Gemini, 20
Geminids, 51
Grus, 23

Halley's Comet, 44
Hercules, 16
Horse's Head Nebula, 34
Horologium, 22
Hydra, 24
Hydrus, 22
Hygeia, 45

Indus, 22

Jupiter, 36, 41

Lacerta, 18
Lagoon Nebula (M8), 28
Leo, 15
Leo Minor, 15
Leonids, 51
Lepus, 21
Libra, 26
light years, 8
Lupus, 26
Lynx, 14
Lyra, 16
Lyrids, 51

Magellanic Clouds, 35
Mare,
    Crisium, 47
    Fecundatis, 47

Frigoris, 47
Humorum, 46
Imbrium, 46
Nectaris, 47
Nubium, 46
Serenitatis, 47
Tranquillitatis, 47
Vaporum, 47
Mars, 36, 40
Mensa, 22
Mercury, 36, 38
meteorites, 51
    iron meteorite, 51
    stony meteorite, 51
meteors, 50
    meteor showers, 50-51
Microscopium, 23
Milky Way, 8, 34
Mira, 33
Mizar, 31
Monoceros, 20
Moon, 9, 46-47
    phases, 48
    eclipse, 49
    halo around the, 52
Musca, 26

Neptune, 37, 43
Nereid, 43
Norma, 26

Oceanus Procellarum, 46
Octans, 22
Orion Nebula, 29
Ophiuchus, 16
Orion, 21
Orionids, 51

Pallas, 45
Pavo, 22
Pegasus, 19
Perseids, 50, 51
Perseus, 18
Phobos, 40
Phoenix, 22
Pictor, 25
Pisces, 18
Piscis Austrinus, 22
Pleiades, 29
Pluto, 37, 43

Praesepe, 28
Proxima Centauri, 8
Puppis, 24
Pyxis, 24

Quadrantids, 41

Reticulum, 22
Rigel, 32

Sagitta, 16
Sagittarius, 26
Saturn, 37, 42
Scorpius, 26
Sculptor, 22
Scutum, 16
Serpens, 17
Sextans, 24
Sirius, 31
Solar System, 8
Southern Cross,
    see Crux
space stations, 53
    Mir, 53
stars, 28, 29, 30, 31, 32, 56
Sun, 8, 32, 36
    eclipse, 49

Taurus, 21
Telescopium, 26
Titan, 42
Triangulum Australe, 26
Triangulum, 18
Triton, 43
Tucana, 22
Tycho, 46

Uranus, 37, 43
Ursa Major, 15
Ursa Minor, 14

Vela, 24
Venus, 36, 39
Vesta, 45
Virgo, 14
Volans, 24
Vulpecula, 16

Zodiac, 37
Zodiacal light, 52

ACKNOWLEDGEMENTS

The publisher would like to thank the
following individuals and organizations:
Cover image: Peter Bull
Illustrations: Gary Bines and Kuo Kang Chen
p10-13 star maps by Karen Webb
Photographs: p1 Digital Vision; p2-3 Digital Vision;
p4-5 Digital Vision; p8 (Sun) Digital Vision;
p28 (Lagoon Nebula) with thanks to NASA; (Praesepe) © by 1998 Wil Milan
(http://www.astrophotographer.com/); p29 (Orion Nebula) Digital Vision;
(Pleiades) D.F. Malin © Royal Observatory, Edinburgh/ AATB; p33 (Antares)
Royal Observatory Edinburgh/ Science Photo Library, (Betelgeuse) with thanks
to NASA; p34 (Horse's Head Nebula) NASA, (Milky Way) Fred Espenak/DODD/
Science Photo Library; p35 (Andromeda Galaxy, Large Magellanic Clouds) Digital
Vision; (Small Magellanic Clouds) Celestial Image Co./ Science Photo Library; p38
US Geological Survey/ Science Photo Library; p36-37 Digital Vision; p39 Digital
Vision; p40 Digital Vision; p41 Digital Vision; p42 Digital Vision; p43 (Neptune and
Uranus) Digital Vision; p44 Digital Vision; p50 (Meteor shower) © V. Winter
(ICSTARS.COM); p51 (iron meteorite) by Carl Allen/ with thanks to NASA, (stony
meteorite) by Cecilia Satterwhite/ with thanks to NASA; p52 (Aurora Borealis)
David Pettitt; (Zodiacal light) © Roger Ressmeyer/Corbis (Halo around the Moon)
© Dennis di Cicco/Corbis; p53 Digital Vision; p54 (Web site images) with thanks to
NASA; p56-57 (photo and backgrounds) Stuart Atkinson
Backgrounds: p6-13, p28-29, p38-43, p46-47, p58-64 Digital Vision